P9-DFP-647

TOMATO SOUP

TOMATO SOUP

THACHER HURD

CROWN PUBLISHERS, INC.
New York

When the lilacs bloom and the swallows return, when the maple trees and oaks grow green with new leaves, then it is planting time on Farmer Clem's farm, far away in the hills.

In the rich brown earth Farmer Clem was planting
his garden. He was planting corn, peas, tomatoes,
zucchini, and brussels sprouts. His cat, George, was
sitting at the edge of the garden with his eyes half-
closed, watching Clem plant.

At the other end of the garden, hidden in the grass, was a tiny yellow house with its own garden. In that garden Father and Mother Mouse were getting ready for their planting.

Father Mouse was rototilling the ground, and Mother Mouse was raking away the stones and smoothing the dirt.

But where
was Baby Mouse?

Mother went upstairs.
"AACHOO! AACHOO!"

"Baby, you have a cold," said Mother. "You have to go to bed."

Poor Baby.

Mother Mouse called the doctor.

"Dr. Wainer? Hello? Baby is sick. Can you come over?"

Dr. Wainer said yes, he would come to look at Baby.

Baby remembered the last time she had been
to the doctor. He had given Baby a shot, and Baby
hadn't liked that. After Mother went back outside,
Baby tiptoed down the stairs . . .

. . . and out the front door. Baby was looking for a place to hide from the doctor.

KACHUNKA KACHUNKA went Father Mouse's rototiller.

"AACHOO!" Baby Mouse sneezed. But the rototiller was so loud that Father and Mother Mouse didn't hear Baby sneeze.

Baby was happy to be out in the warm air. She tiptoed through the grass and into Farmer Clem's garden. Baby Mouse watched Farmer Clem plant his garden.

Then she saw a bag of seeds lying on the ground. Baby looked inside.

Baby thought that would be a
good place to hide from the doctor.
She crawled inside the bag of seeds.
Then Baby sneezed.

George, the cat, opened his eyes wide. He was interested in a bag that sneezed.

George crept up to the bag and picked it up. He started walking out of the garden. Baby was trapped!

"Hey!" yelled Farmer Clem. "Come back with my seeds!"

Clem ran after George. George scampered across
the garden and under the barn.
Farmer Clem's pigs were amazed.

When he was safely under the barn, George stuck
his nose into the bag.

All of a sudden Baby sneezed again.

SPLUNK! A kernel of corn stuck in George's nose.

Now it was George's turn to sneeze.

Baby Mouse scampered out from under the barn . . .

. . . and ran across the barnyard.
George was right behind.

George pounced.

SMUSH!

George fell into

the onions and rotten tomatoes

and potato peelings

in the pigs' trough.

The pigs were amazed.

Poor George.

Baby was hungry. She started for home. Baby hoped that the doctor had come and gone.

"Baby!" said Mother and Father Mouse when they saw her. "Where have you been? You should be in bed! The doctor is coming soon."

Mother tucked Baby back in bed, and Father brought her some tomato soup.

Soon, Dr. Wainer drove up in his truck.

"Poor Baby," said Mother Mouse as she opened the
door to Baby's room. "Baby?"
Where was Baby now?

She was hiding under the covers.

Dr. Wainer took out his stethoscope and listened to Baby's chest.

"Don't worry," said Dr. Wainer, "it's just a cold. Take this medicine every four hours and you'll feel much better."

No shot! That made Baby happy.

Until she tasted the medicine.

"BLEEACCH!"

Dr. Wainer patted Baby on the head.

"You'll feel better soon," he said.

Dr. Wainer went downstairs and had a cup of coffee with Father and Mother.

Dr. Wainer waved good-bye as he went out the front door. Just then something came flying out of Baby's window . . .

. . . and landed on Dr. Wainer's head. It was the bottle of medicine.

"I'm so sorry!" cried Mother when she saw Dr. Wainer's smashed hat.

"Oh, it's nothing," said Dr. Wainer. "Just make sure that Baby takes her medicine."

"Try to be more careful!" said Mother as she
brought the bottle of medicine back to Baby's room.
Then she tucked Baby into bed and went downstairs.

Baby felt sleepy, but she heard something outside her window.

It was George again. He looked hungry. And he
was creeping closer and closer to the Mouse house.
Baby looked down at George. Then she smiled.

Baby opened her bottle of medicine. She leaned
out the window and *SPLIRT!*

She poured all the medicine on George's head!

"MMRROWWWRRGGRRAACCKK!" George
yowled, and he ran home as fast as he could.

"YUCK!" said Farmer Clem. "What did you get into, George? You smell like a skunk in a pigs' trough." Then Farmer Clem gave George a tomato-juice bath to get rid of that awful smell.

Poor George. He hated baths.

Meanwhile, back at the Mouse house, it was bedtime.

And it was time for Baby's medicine.

Mother Mouse opened the bottle.

"What happened to all the medicine?" Mother asked Baby.

Baby didn't say a word.

And the next day she felt much better.

For the real Dr. Wainer

Copyright © 1992 by Thacher Hurd
All rights reserved. No part of this book may be reproduced or transmitted in any form or by any means, electronic or mechanical, including photocopying, recording, or by any information storage and retrieval system, without permission in writing from the publisher.

Published by Crown Publishers, Inc., a Random House company, 225 Park Avenue South, New York, New York 10003
CROWN is a trademark of Crown Publishers, Inc.
Manufactured in Hong Kong
Library of Congress Cataloging-in-Publication Data
Hurd, Thacher.
Tomato soup / Thacher Hurd. p.   cm.
Summary: When Baby Mouse catches a cold, she finds a mischievous way to avoid taking her medicine. [1. Sick—Fiction. 2. Medicine—Fiction. 3. Mice—Fiction.] I. Title.
PZ7.H9562To 1991 [E]—dc20   90-21421
ISBN 0-517-58237-6 (trade)
     0-517-58238-4 (lib. bdg.)   10 9 8 7 6 5 4 3 2 1   First Edition